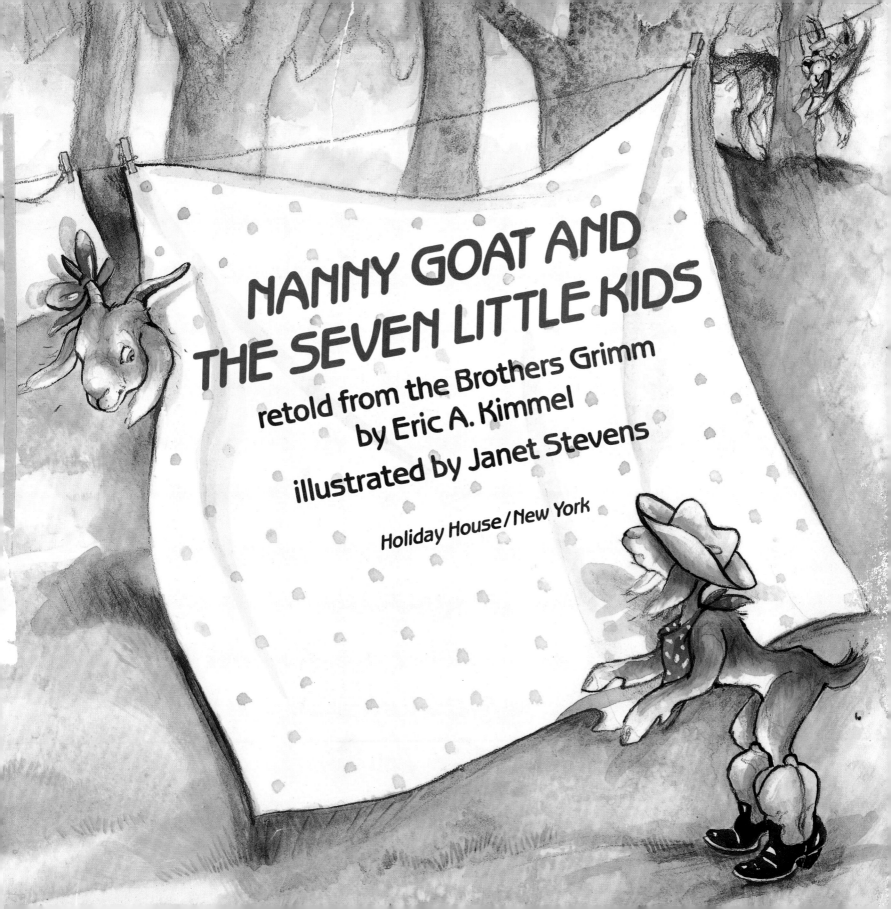

NANNY GOAT AND THE SEVEN LITTLE KIDS

retold from the Brothers Grimm
by Eric A. Kimmel

illustrated by Janet Stevens

Holiday House/New York

Library of Congress Cataloging-in-Publication Data

Kimmel, Eric A.
Nanny goat and the seven little kids / retold from the Brothers
Grimm by Eric A. Kimmel ; illustrations by Janet Stevens.
p.   cm.
Summary: Mother goat rescues her seven kids after they are
swallowed by a wicked wolf.
ISBN 0-8234-0789-6
[1. Fairy tales.   2. Folklore—Germany.]   I. Grimm, Wilhelm,
1786–1859.   II. Grimm, Jacob, 1785–1863.   III. Stevens, Janet, ill.
IV. Title.
PZ8.K527Nan   1990
398.24′5297358′0943—dc20
[E]   89-20058   CIP   AC
ISBN 0-8234-0789-6

Once upon a time, there was a nanny goat who lived in a little house in the forest with her children, seven little kids. The kids were as good as good can be, and they loved their mother dearly.

One day, the nanny goat put on her hat and gloves.
"Children," she said, "I am going to the market to buy
some vegetables for our supper. Before I leave, there is
something I must warn you about. The big bad wolf has
been seen in the neighborhood. Be watchful and wary while
I am gone. Never, never, never let the big bad wolf into the
house, for if the big bad wolf gets into the house, he will eat
you all up!"

"Oh, Mother, do not fear!" the seven little kids promised. "We will never, never, never let the big bad wolf into the house."

Then the nanny goat kissed them all good-bye, slipped her basket over her arm, and started down the road to the market. As soon as she was out of sight, the seven little kids locked the door and bolted it tight.

Now someone was watching from behind the big oak tree. It was the big bad wolf! And his mouth began to water at the thought of those nice, fat, tender, tasty, juicy little kids.

The moment the nanny goat was out of sight, he ran up to the little house and pounded on the door.

"Who's there?" cried the seven little kids.

"IT'S I, YOUR MOTHER!" the big bad wolf said in his rough, harsh voice. "OPEN THE DOOR AND LET ME IN!"

The seven little kids laughed. "You're not our mother! Our mother has a soft, sweet voice; not a rough, harsh voice like yours. You're the big bad wolf, and we won't let you into the house!"

"Curses!" the big bad wolf growled. He turned around and ran all the way back through the forest until he reached his cave.

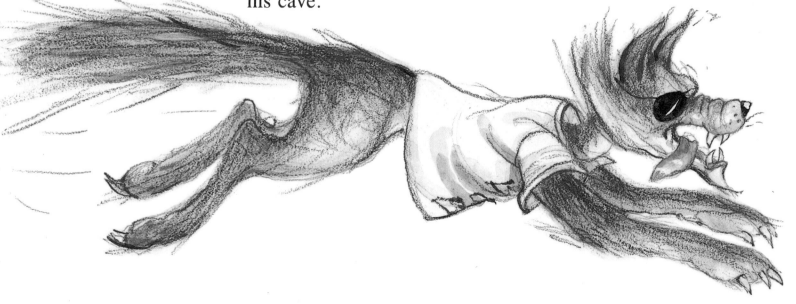

There he took a piece of chalk, chewed it, and swallowed it. The chalk made his voice soft and sweet.

Then he ran all the way back to the little house. This time he knocked gently on the door.

"Who's there?" cried the seven little kids.

"It is I, your mother," the big bad wolf said in his soft, sweet voice. "Please open the door and let me in."

The seven little kids couldn't decide what to do. Whoever was at the door did have a soft, sweet voice like Mother. But Mother said she was going to the market and wouldn't be home till suppertime. Was it really Mother? How could they be sure? The oldest little kid had an idea.

"Come to the window and show us your feet," she said.

The big bad wolf came to the window and held up his horrible, hairy feet. The seven little kids took one look and laughed.

"You're not our mother! Our mother has pretty white feet, not horrible, hairy ones. You're the big bad wolf, and we won't let you into the house!"

Then, standing on his front paws, the big bad wolf ran all the way back to the little house. Once again he knocked on the door.

"Who's there?" cried the seven little kids.

"It is I, your mother," said the big bad wolf in his soft, sweet voice. "Please open the door and let me in."

As soon as he reached his cave, he took a big bar of soap and scrubbed and scrubbed his horrible, hairy feet until they were clean and bright. Then he took the nail scissors and clipped his cruel, curved claws. When that was done he dipped his feet into the flour barrel right up to the knees to make them pretty and soft and white.

Then, standing on his front paws, the big bad wolf ran all the way back to the little house. Once again he knocked on the door.

"Who's there?" cried the seven little kids.

"It is I, your mother," said the big bad wolf in his soft, sweet voice. "Please open the door and let me in."

"Come to the window and show us your feet," she said.

The big bad wolf came to the window and held up his horrible, hairy feet. The seven little kids took one look and laughed.

"You're not our mother! Our mother has pretty white feet, not horrible, hairy ones. You're the big bad wolf, and we won't let you into the house!"

"Curses!" The big bad wolf turned around and ran all the
way back through the forest.

"First come to the window and show us your feet," said the seven little kids. The big bad wolf came to the window and held up his horrible, hairy feet which were now pretty and soft and white. The seven little kids took one look and said, "Whoever is at the door does have a soft, sweet voice like Mother. And whoever is at the window does have pretty white feet like Mother. It must be Mother, come home from the market early. Mother dear, come in, come in!"

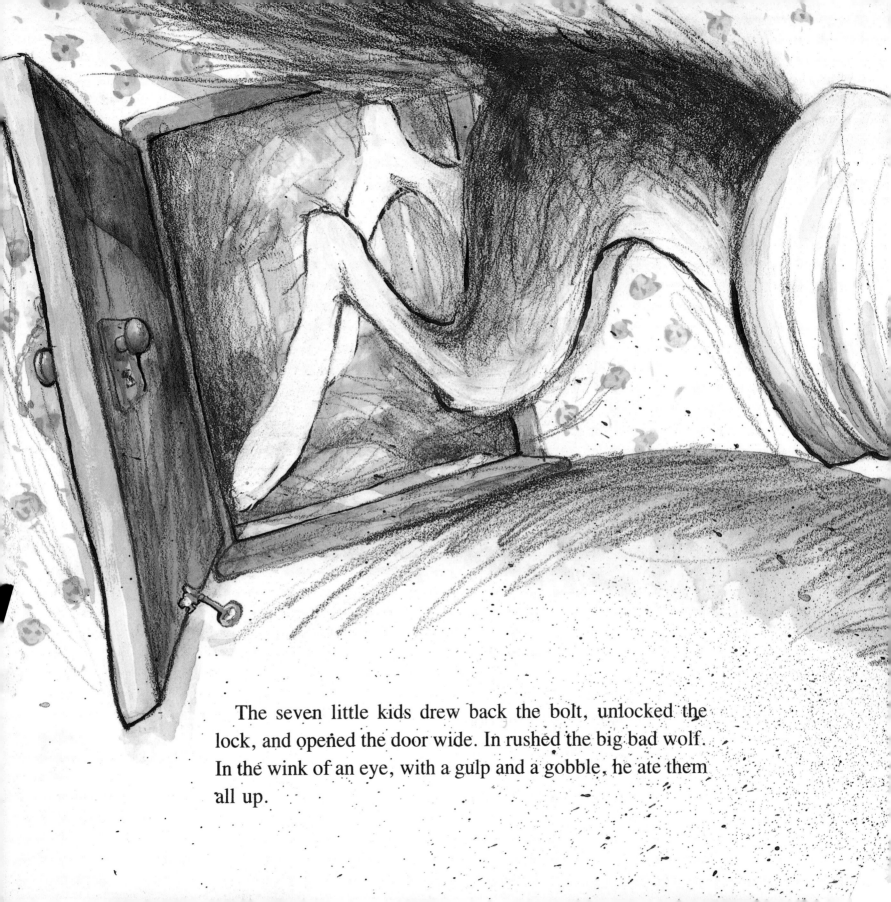

The seven little kids drew back the bolt, unlocked the lock, and opened the door wide. In rushed the big bad wolf. In the wink of an eye, with a gulp and a gobble, he ate them all up.

Even so, that greedy wolf still wasn't satisfied. He hid
beneath the kitchen table, so that when the nanny goat
returned from the market with her arms full of groceries, up
jumped the big bad wolf and ate her up, too!

By now the big bad wolf began to feel very full and very sleepy. "What a delicious supper!" he said with a yawn.

He started back home through the forest. But he only got as far as the rushing stream. By then he was so tired and so sleepy he couldn't go another step. He lay down beneath a spreading tree, closed his eyes, and was soon sound asleep.

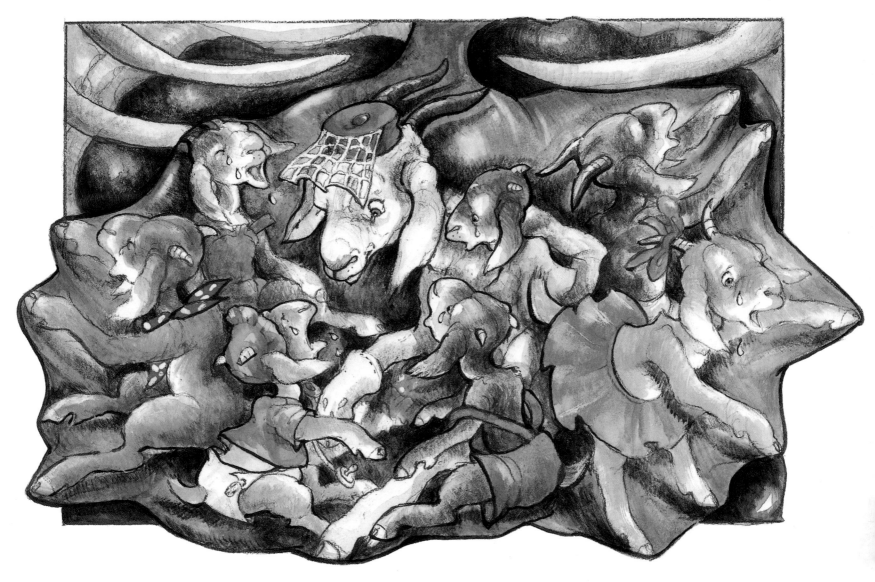

Meanwhile, inside the big bad wolf's stomach, the seven little kids were crying.

"Oh, Mother, please forgive us! We didn't mean to disobey. The big bad wolf was cleverer than we thought. He made his voice soft and sweet like yours; he made his feet pretty and white like yours. We thought it was you and let him in. Now he has eaten us all up! Whatever shall we do?"

"Hush, children. Dry your eyes," the nanny goat said. "All is not lost. That big bad wolf is not half so clever as he thinks." She reached into her apron and took out her sewing scissors, the ones with the sharp points. With these she made a tiny hole in the big bad wolf's stomach, just big

enough for the littlest kid to jump through. Then she made
the hole a little bigger, just big enough for the next littlest
kid to jump through; and a little bigger; and a little bigger
until the hole was big enough for all the little kids to jump
through as well as for the nanny goat herself to jump
through, too.

When that was done, the nanny goat gathered all her
children around and said to them, "I want you each to go
and find a stone as big as yourself and bring it here." The
seven little kids hurried to find stones as big as themselves
while the nanny goat found a stone as big as she. One by
one, the nanny goat took the stones and put them inside the

big bad wolf's stomach. With her needle and thread she sewed up the stomach with a seam so fine, the wolf would never know he had been cut open. Then the nanny goat and the seven little kids ran all the way back to their little house, locked the door, and bolted it tight.

An hour later, the big bad wolf woke up. "Oh!" he groaned. "I don't feel so good. It feels like I ate eight big stones instead of eight juicy goats. Oh! I feel terrible. What can I do?" Then he thought, "Perhaps a drink of cool water will help settle my stomach."

The big bad wolf tottered over to the rushing stream. He bent down to drink, but just then the stones inside his stomach shifted. With a great splash, the big bad wolf fell into the rushing stream. The heavy stones carried him to the bottom. He must have liked it down there because he never came back.

From that day on, the nanny goat and the seven little kids never had to worry about the big bad wolf again. And they lived happily ever after.